Where's the Dinosaur?

Illustrated by Keith Moseley

George received a letter from his grandfather saying he had some exciting news.

"Hurry!" Grandfather called as he filled a balloon with supplies. "We are going on a long voyage. I'll explain everything on the way!"

Soon Grandfather, George, and Meg the dog rose high into the sky.

"We're heading for a remote island many hundreds of miles away," Grandfather explained. "There are rumors of dinosaurs still living there."

"Of course, rumors are one thing and facts are another," he added. "I'll only believe it if I witness those dinosaurs for myself, right in front of my nose!"

At last they approached the island.
It was a mysterious, swampy land
with a large volcano in the middle.
It looked just like the kind of place
where dinosaurs would live.

George and Meg noticed some strange creatures following them. "Can some dinosaurs fly, Grandfather?" George asked. But Grandfather was too busy looking through his telescope. "If there are dinosaurs down there," he told himself firmly, "then I'll be sure to find them!"

Their balloon drifted gently down into a clearing.
"A dinosaur egg!" George cried excitedly.

"I'm afraid not," Grandfather advised, "otherwise the mother would be nearby." He was too busy talking to notice that the mother dinosaur was watching right behind him.

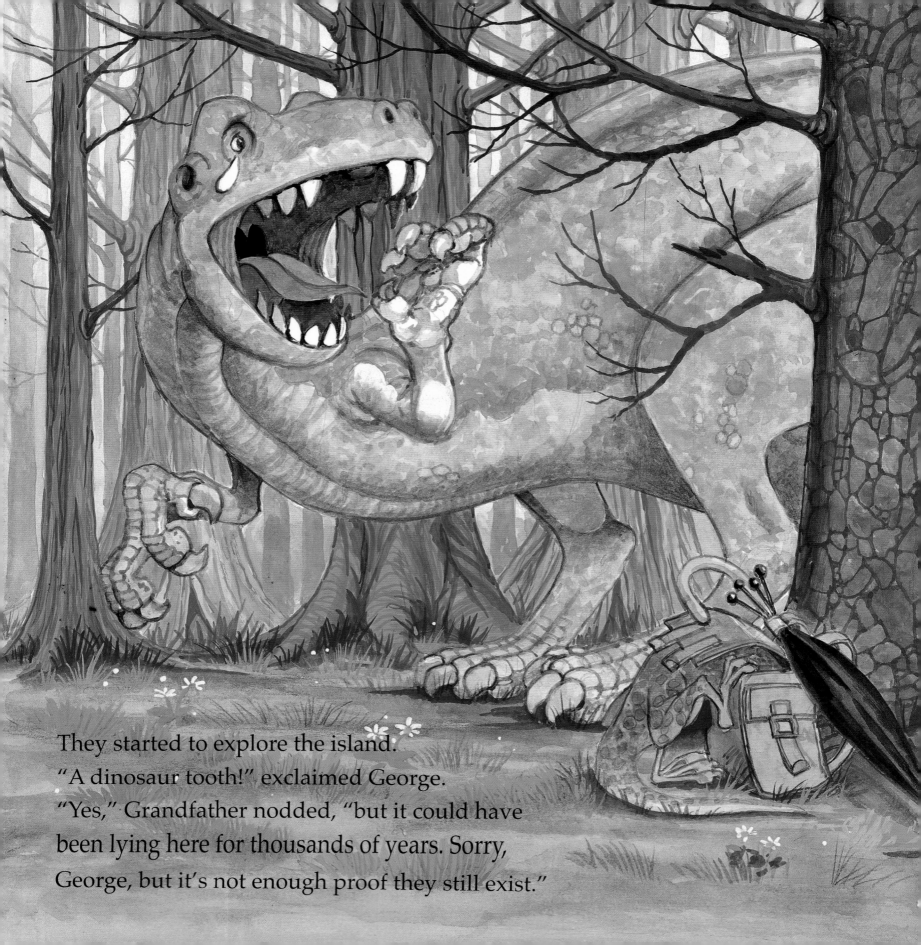

They started to explore the island.
"A dinosaur tooth!" exclaimed George.
"Yes," Grandfather nodded, "but it could have
been lying here for thousands of years. Sorry,
George, but it's not enough proof they still exist."

Later when they came across some
up-rooted trees, George exclaimed,
"There must be dinosaurs living here!"
But Grandfather still was not convinced.
"It might have just been a fierce storm," he said.

When they found a good place to rest for the night, Grandfather made a cozy camp fire. Suddenly, someone's tummy started to rumble very, very loudly. It wasn't George's tummy, nor Meg's. "Nor mine," said Grandfather. "It must be that volcano rumbling over there!"

The next morning they continued to explore. George wanted Grandfather to examine the bones nearby. But Grandfather shook his head with disappointment. "Unfortunately, there's no proof at all that any dinosaurs are still alive on this island."

Grandfather had an idea and clambered up a nearby tree.

"I'll have a really good view from the top," he shouted down.
"If there are any dinosaurs hiding from us in the forest, they
won't be able to outwit me!"

Grandfather searched far and wide from the top of the tree, but, sadly, there wasn't a single dinosaur to be seen.

They journeyed farther into the forest.
Grandfather looked everywhere for dinosaur
evidence, determined not to miss even the
slightest clue. But he could find nothing at all.

As they started their long flight home, Grandfather remarked sadly, "What a shame. Not a single dinosaur to be seen!" Then he added proudly, "You see, you can't believe rumors!"

Grandfather did not spot any dinosaurs but did you?
How many did you count during the story?
George has the answer when he goes to meet Grandfather.
Can you find that too?